Also by Martine Leavitt

Keturah and Lord Death
Heck Superhero
Tom Finder
The Dollmage
The Taker's Key
The Prism Moon
The Dragon's Tapestry

MY BOOK OF LIFE BY ANGEL

MY BOOK OF LIFE BY ANGEL

MARTINE LEAVITT

GROUNDWOOD BOOKS
HOUSE OF ANANSI PRESS
TORONTO

Chapter headings are quoted from *Paradise Lost* by John Milton, Modern Library edition, 2008, edited by William Kerrigan, John Rumrich and Stephen M. Fallon.

Groundwood Books/ House of Anansi Press
110 Spadina Avenue, Suite 801, Toronto, Ontario M5V 2K4

We acknowledge for their financial support of our publishing program the Canada Council for the Arts, the Government of Canada through the Canada Book Fund (CBF) and the Ontario Arts Council.

 Canada Council Conseil des Arts
for the Arts du Canada **ONTARIO ARTS COUNCIL**
CONSEIL DES ARTS DE L'ONTARIO

Library and Archives Canada Cataloguing in Publication

Leavitt, Martine
My book of life by Angel / Martine Leavitt.

Issued also in electronic format.
ISBN 978-1-55498-117-5

I. Title.

PS8573.E323M9 2012   jC813'.54   C2012-902715-4

Cover illustration by Anna + Elena = Balbusso (www.balbusso.com)

Groundwood Books is committed to protecting our natural environment. As part of our efforts, the interior of this book is printed on paper that contains 100% post-consumer recycled fibers, is acid-free and is processed chlorine-free.

Printed and bound in Canada

 MIX
Paper from
responsible sources
FSC
www.fsc.org **FSC® C004071**

 **ANCIENT FOREST** ™
FRIENDLY

For the families of the Eastside angels

Bid her well beware . . .

When Serena went missing
I looked in all the places she might go
and she wasn't anywhere,
just like a lot of the other girls weren't anywhere.

I thought oh no
when Serena didn't show up at her corner one night
and not the next night or the next,
and then she didn't show up to church Wednesday.
She always went to church Wednesday
and told her man Asia it was for free hot dogs
but it was really for church—
she told me that secret.

Once a man came
who smelled so bad everybody pulled away,
but Serena said, welcome, you are with friends,
have a hot dog.

She said she picked me to love
because of my name Angel and because of my face,
but then she loved me just because.
She said that.

She said her heart's desire was to see an angel.
She said, if I could see an angel
that would mean I'm still God's little girl.

She said,
Angel, if you get scared sometime
on a bad date,
do this—

She stared big-eyed at nothing over my head
and said,
angel, angel . . .

I laughed, said, you see an angel?

She said, no not yet,
but just saying it or thinking about one
has powers.

Really, Serena? I said.
Ha ha really?
you think there is such a thing as angels?

She said soft, maybe.

But she meant yes really.

The first time Call told me
to get out there
and me scared and not knowing anything
and Call watching from the café across the street
saying no more candy for free—
that first time Serena said, I'll tell you what I know.

She said, your eyes be always on the man
you don't have eyes for anyone but him
you don't have business with anybody but him—
that's the only way he can stand it,
if you aren't alive except when he needs you to be.
Serena taught me about drinks and dinner,
told me how to make it go fast, how to fake it.

She said, and don't you forget
your name suits you.

When she wasn't at church Wednesday
I said, Asia, where is she?
He said, she's run out on me.

I thought, but did not say,
she gave me her running-away money
to hide under my mattress
and it is still there.

Last church Wednesday
Serena said to me,
Angel, you write about Nena
who had a pretty house
and pretty parents
and was a ten minute walk from Micky D's.

One day she didn't go home for supper
and then she didn't go home for curfew
and then she didn't go home.
Nena went for a burger
and ended up at Hastings and Main.

Her man, the one who found her, lonesome,
said to his friends,
it's the ones from good homes
who follow orders best—
it's the ones from good families
who have the best social skills,
who never learned how to fight—
they make the best money.

Serena said to me,
tell the story of Connie
who said, I'm leaving the life behind,
who said, I'm going to testify against the man
who brought me here and dogged me awful.
She said, I'm going to protect other girls
and get that boy in jail.

On courtroom day, there he was,
wearing a pink tie,
and in every seat of the courtroom
were his buddies,
saying with eyes,
if he goes down,
so do you.

Write how Connie failed to prove to the judge
that she was in imminent and present danger
so her man walked away
and Connie got found dead
strangled by a pink tie.

Serena said,
John the john has made you read that poem,
has taught you fancy words and fancy grammar—
Angel, you tell about Blood Alley
and Pigeon Park—
the cardboard tents
and the water rats
and the delousing showers,
the SROs and the cockroaches,
the people drinking out of puddles
and all the girls going missing . . .

Tell all that, Angel.

I said no.

She said yes.

I said no.

She said yes.

I said no that is dumb.

Then Serena didn't show at church Wednesday, and I got a book to write in.

I stopped to listen to the street preacher
who talked about God's top ten
and how everything you do is recorded in a book of life
and angels will read from it someday.
Is this what you want your story to be? he said.
Is this what you want everyone to hear?

I imagined that,
to hear everything about me
read out loud by an angel
like I used to read to my little brother Jeremy.

I held my notebook
and wished I could write my story over
and in this new story I gave up Call's candy forever
and I called my dad and he came and got me
and him and me and Jeremy
drove away from Call forever,
and when we got there,
there would be Serena.

So I tried to make it come true.
I called Dad from the pay phone near the library
and it was sorry this number is no longer in service
so I wrote him a letter and even mailed it,
saying,
Serena my friend is missing
I am cleaning up my act like you said
and I vow my deepest vow
that I won't take Call's candy forever.

I wrote on the front of my book
My Book of Life by Angel
Which Is My Real Name,
and This Is My Real Story
for Maybe an Angel to Read.

I wrote in my book,
Serena, when you come back
I will tell you about my vow
and my letter to Dad
and I am sorry I laughed at your idea of angels,
I want an angel too.

I wrote
my angel wouldn't be one of the long dead
who has forgotten being alive,
who is used to sitting on a throne
and being buddies with God.

My angel would be a fresh-dead one,
still longing for chocolate cake,
still wishing she could come back
and find out who won American Idol.

That's the one I want—
just a junior one
who might not mind saving
a girl like me.

Subtle he needs must be, who could
seduce angels . . .

In the Vancouver Downtown Eastside,
where Call lives and now me too,
all the doors and windows are barred at night—
the street is the jail
and there's no escape.

Where Call lives
people know how to sleep sitting up
and how to eat without teeth
and how to carry their whole world
on their backs.

Where Call lives
most of the churches are shelters,
with beds for the bedless
and soup for the soupless.

Call has a good haircut and good shoes—
shoes with laces double-knotted and hard soles
and stiff heels
and pockets in his shirts—
he could walk into an office
and nobody would blink.

But here they blink.
Here, he is gentry.
He says, I am the beginning of gentrification
at Hastings and Main.

Call wants to be the boss of something.
He can't do it in the real world
so he will be the king of Eastside.
He is always disappointed with Eastside.
It lets him down every day.

I met Call because of shoes,
because I stole shoes.
No—shoe,
just the one on display,
the one everyone touches, picks up,
tries to stuff their foot into,
the one people say, oooh that is so sweet,
or,
why would anybody want that?

Serena said once,
Angel, shoes are going to be the death of you.

My mom died of holes.
People who get cancer can feel lumps,
but my mom felt spaces, holes—
she couldn't explain it better.

The doctor said she had osteoporosis,
but Mom said she had holes in her bones.
She said her memory was bad
because of the holes in her brain
and she would laugh.

Then she died of a hole in her heart
she had since she was born
but nobody knew.

Serena said,
that put a hole in you, Angel,
which you tried to fill up with Call.

After Mom died, Dad hated our house.
He kept hearing Mom on the stairs
and in the kitchen
and turning over in bed—
he knew her ghost was playing hide and seek with him
and never letting him win.

Dad said, we're moving,
and Jeremy said, where?
And Dad said, anywhere,
but he never did
because sometimes in the closet
he could smell her.

After Mom died
I started to run away from home,
but just to the mall.
I liked the shoe stores best at the mall.
High-heeled shoes meant walking pretty,
meant looking good in a getaway way,
meant strutting your stuff, being tough.
At the mall
I made myself up as I went.
I pretended in lipstick.

Then I got caught
and Dad had to come pick me up
at the police station.

I tried not to anymore,
but then there was that periwinkle pump
with the yellow strap
and he had to come pick me up again.
And again.
Dad didn't know what to do with me,
stealing shoe and getting caught.
He kept saying, I don't know what to do with you—

but Call did.

Every day after school
I pretended to run away to the mall.
I pretended the bookstore was my home
and the leather reading chairs were my chairs
and the bookstore clerk was my aunt who loved to see me read.

I pretended the cinnamon bun smell
was Mom making them for me
and the clothing stores were my walk-in closets
and the ice cream place was my freezer
and the bathroom was my bathroom
and I lived at the mall.

Once in a while I would go to my pretend closet
and take just one shoe,
just pick it like a fruit off a tree.

One day I picked up a pink peekaboo
and slipped it in my backpack, and just then—
Call.

He said, hey, I saw you.
I saw what you did,
don't be scared, your secret's safe with me.
You hungry? he asked.
Buy you something.
C'mon, don't be scared, I'm just Call, I'm okay.

I said no
and he said, then I'll have to turn you in.
He smiled when he said it
but I let him buy me Chinese
and he laughed when I told him about my collection.
You think anyone really cares about one shoe? he said,
and suddenly nothing seemed so bad.

I said, thanks for the food, I've got to go.
He said, see you later diddle diddle dumpling.
I said, what?
And he said, later.

Every day I came
and every day he was there.

I said, don't you have to go to college?
to work?
how old are you?

He said, I'm a businessman.

What kind of business?

Renewable resources, he said.

What's that?

You ask a lot of questions, he said.

Call bought me fried chicken and cinnamon buns
and told me I was pretty,
said I had a sweet tooth in my sweet face,
listened to me about Mom,
kept saying, I know how it is,
come with me, be my girl,
we'll travel the world.
But I didn't go that day
or the next
or the next
because I crazy loved my little brother Jeremy.

And then Call said,
you wanna fly, Angel?
He said, you want candy for that sweet tooth of yours?

At first it was so fun, Call's candy,
and all the missing of Mom went away
and I was all
        I'm so baby uptown
        I'm so baby bless my soul
        I'm so baby high heels
        I'm so baby rock and roll.

        I'm so spinning pretty pretty pat pat .
        Little bit of this and a little bit of that that.

        I'm so baby sheek sheek
        I'm so baby got control

I'm so baby hot walk
I'm so baby on a roll.

I'm so honey dance with me
Little bit o' la-la, little bit o' tee-hee . . .

One day when I was on a sugar high
I brought it home and Dad wasn't there
and Jeremy was and he thought I was so funny.
We danced and I gave him lots of school advice
like keep your pencils pointy
and ask your teacher how her weekend was.
Then Dad.
Dad was there
and he saw how it was
with all my sugar right there on the table
and he said, what are you doing?
what are you doing?
and I said, I don't know I don't know
I'm sorry I'm sorry.
But sorry wasn't enough for how mad he was
and he yelled until I was too mad to be sorry
and I could see Dad was too sad about Mom
to be sad about me
and I watched his eyes give up as we shouted
until Jeremy cried and I stopped.

Dad watched me pack with given-up eyes
and watched me walk away.
He said, don't come home till you clean up your act.

Call took me to his apartment.
He said, you can stay as long as you like,
said, you don't need school.
So I stayed
and I didn't even know I'd run away.

That was in September.
Now it is May.
I did not know how long it had been
since I came to Call's place.
He does not have calendars.

I found out when I called to report Serena missing
and the police lady said,
when did you see her last?
I said, last church Wednesday
and she said, May 17 then,
and I said, May?
I said, I would like to report nine months missing
ha ha.

She didn't laugh,
and I hung up.

In Call's place the couch's bones were broken,
its skin covered in scars and sores.
I should have known right away, looking at that couch.

I felt like I'd gone into free fall
and fell all the way down to the bottom
and found a whole place down there.

Call became my pretend first boyfriend
and gave me my first kiss.
I didn't feel anything, but I let him,
kept thinking, hey, I'm kissing! I'm kissing!

I told him about my Jeremy and that I crazy loved him.
He said, you have a little brother? and he smiled.

I thought, wow, he likes kids.

After a while
Call said, Angel do you love me?
I said yes.
But do you really love me?
And I said yes.
Would you do anything for me?
And I said
yes
yes.

Now I know
in a single breath of yes, yes,
you can hear your soul
leaking out of your mouth.
A yes can change you inside,
make all the rules go sky-why-not . . .

All those clothes and dinners
and all that candy—
Call said, I'm out of cash,
can you help me out?
do you really love me?

At first it was just to be nice to a friend . . .
and then a friend of a friend . . .

As soon as I knew what Call had made me,
the first time a man said in a word what I was
and I couldn't even say that's not true—
as soon as that happened

I knew I could not bring that word home
even if I wanted to—
Jeremy and I weren't even allowed to say stupid
or hate—
my dad would never allow a word like me.

I found out Call's candy flies you down
tips you inside out
dumps you upside down
flies you through empty space
to the black hole in the middle of you
and you can't stop
can't stop
unless you want to vomit up whole planets . . .

I thought I hated my dad—
I thought he was mean,
treating me like a baby,
and I never told him where I was,
never called him
so he would worry.

But I didn't know what mean was
until I found out the real Call.

That one word yes
gave Call all my words—
he knew when I said yes
that he would have my voice in a bottle,
that no one would hear me
again.

Innocence, that as a veil had shadowed them
from knowing ill, was gone . . .

I woke up in the night
and it was dark and the beginning of my day.

Call said, wake up Angel,
all the other girls are out there earning for their men,
man I wish I had a girl like that,
if only you loved me like that.

I was awake so fast,
looking for my shoes
only ones, no pairs.
My clothes were squashed to one side of the closet—
Call's clothes took up all the space—
but my shoes covered the closet floor
and hid under the bed
and were piled at the door.

My face was hot
and the rest of me cold
my hips out of joint
my eyeballs filled with acid
and I thought, here I go,
and when Call said, I've got candy, good stuff for my girl,
I thought yes
and then I thought about my letter and my vow,
and I said ever so polite, no thank you.

He said, why, because of Serena?
He said, you won't last long,
you don't know how bad it can get.

He said, don't make me wake you up again.

I picked out a pink ballet shoe
and an apple green sandal
and Call said,
I called some of the gentry for a meeting
at All-Night Kayos—they've got pork ribs on special
and I've got an announcement.
Meet me there after.

I wanted to say
okay okay give me candy,
so I can be floatable while I work,
but I didn't.
I didn't.

I went downstairs and through the store,
Slingin' Ink Tattoo Parlour, to go out.

Tattoo—he's the owner—
stared after me
wanting to needlework me,
wishing I could be his canvas.

He grabbed my arm, said,
don't you wanna be my art?
won't you let me choose?
not just copy some picture off the wall
but something out of my own head?

But Call says I'm supposed to be innocent,
clean baby-girl skin
no makeup
so dates can paste on any face they want
and I can tell new dates it's my first time
and I am thirteen even though I am sixteen.
Sixteen doesn't make as much money
as thirteen.
Serena was nineteen,
told dates she was sixteen,
told me she was a hundred down there.

Tattoo whispered to me,
I know what you are,
said, your skin could be the way
they know I'm alive.

I said, I am scared of needles, let go,
but Tattoo squeezed my arm hard, harder—

I remembered Serena's tip
about staring and saying, angel, angel—

so I did.
I looked past Tattoo
and said, angel, angel,
and he let go
and spun around
thinking it was Call.
It wasn't Call
and it wasn't an angel either
but I got away.

Serena would have said, see?
That's what saying angel does.

I passed the Carnegie library
at the corner of Hastings and Main,
which has a message board
and stained-glass windows,
one of John Milton.

I had never heard of John Milton
until John the john found me
and became one of my regulars.
He gets me to read him paradise lost
by John Milton, book nine, only book nine,
while he does his thing.
Call said, poetry, that is twisted,
but okay because he pays so good.

The pay phone is the border
between Eastside and Chinatown—
I walked past
and just like that
I was in China.

I passed the Jimi Hendrix shrine
fenced in an alley,
fake grass and plastic flowers
and posters of Jimi
and his music playing
and Jimi singing about angels coming down from heaven
and staying for tea and stories—

I thought, that's what happens
when you start looking for an angel.

I walked to my corner
at the gate of ten thousand happinesses
and I stared at my shoes while I walked,
stared at them walking me there again.
That's how I get to my corner
at the gate of ten thousand happinesses
every time.

I stood on the kiddie corner
where I always do,
just a line in the sidewalk
between me and the midtrack.

Widow works the midtrack
on the other side of the line.
Widow waits for men
who are not into little girls like me.
She says, at least I'm not a lowtrack girl.

Widow says to me all the time,
I don't feel anything
care anything
it's just a big whatever—
I've got the menu memorized
makes no nevermind to me
who cares?

But she cares if I cross the line in the sidewalk.

Widow yells at me if I come too close
but she and I talk
on our own sides of the line.

I said to Widow,
do you think an angel really came to Jimi Hendrix?
I heard him singing about it in a song,
an angel coming for tea.
That would be cool if an angel came to me ...

Widow laughed,
she thinks I am so funny,
laughed and said,
we're the last ones on earth who would get an angel.

I thought, maybe the last ones on earth
are the ones they come to.

You can think about stuff like that when you're waiting,
when you don't work by sun
when you have a little dark to stand in
some moonlight to walk in
ankle deep down the street
so no one sees your mismatched shoes.

When Widow wasn't looking I leaned back
so my face didn't go over the line, not my nose or chin,
and I stretched my toe right over her line,
the line between kiddie corner and midtrack.
She didn't even look at me,
she just knew,
yelled,
you watch out for that toe,
one night I'll cut it off.

How did she know?

She talks like that, but she watches out for me.
She has always helped me out
just like Serena did
only not as nice.

Two men walked by Widow and said,
I wouldn't take that for free.
They said, hey ugly,
they said, waste of oxygen that one.

Widow, she stood like a queen,
back straight, chin up, silent,
breathing oxygen,
looking hot.

After the men were gone
I said, Widow, how do you keep your figure?
you look so good . . .
She said, the Jenny Crack diet
and she cracked up.

And then the tourists came out—
Widow calls them hoons—
rich kids, kids with cars
who want to see the poorest postal code in the country.
They threw things at us
        bleach
        spitballs
        eggs.
I said, ignore them, don't pay attention.
I willed her with my eyes to have dignity.
I said, I'm thinking angel, angel, which has powers.
They won't touch you.
And they didn't—everything fell at our feet.

Serena would have said,
see? see?

Widow said to me, you are a freak.
She said, don't you step over that line.

A van with tinted windows drove by, slowed,
and Widow called, hey Angel! come here!
So I walked toward her and the van moved on.

As soon as it was gone
Widow said, hey, stay on your side of the line,
and I said, but you called me,
and she said, don't you get into that van
and don't think I care if you do.
Widow said, I got a bad feeling about that van.
She said, pay attention—
you wanna be the next one to go missing?

Widow said, everyone on the street is saying there's a killer
but the police say no.

She talked about a Mr. P,
who she has heard whispers about,
and how Mr. P has a van.

It is true girls are missing. That part is true.
Not just Serena.

Widow told me Debra is missing—
she played guitar and piano
and sang like Janis Joplin
and dreamed of going to Nashville.
Dawn is missing—
her father died with his head in her lap when she was five.
Dianne is missing—
she was a nurse's aide who couldn't support all her kids
and welfare wouldn't help
because she had a job and too many kids
because they don't pay for that many kids.

I said to Widow
Call says in the business
girls go missing all the time
and it doesn't mean a thing.
They run away or they go to rehab
or they go to jail or they get sick—

Widow said, Dianne would have called her kids.
She's not missing, she's dead,
someone killed her,
you think about that.

I said, don't worry, Widow, you are safe with me around.

She said, just because your name is Angel
doesn't mean angels are real.
She said, I'm an atheist thank God.

I said, Widow maybe you have had a traumatic experience.

She said, I'll give you a traumatic experience,
said, I bet Angel's not your real name anyway.

I said, it is hard to believe but try.
I said, Widow what is your real name?

She said, guess.

So I said,
Linda?
Susan?
Debra?
Janice?
Kimberly?
Maxine?
What is it, then?

She said, no, no, no,
and her face turned from mad to sad.

She said,
I don't remember.

I wish I could remember.
And then she was mad again,
said,
why do all the crazies come here,
you keep your sweet baby face out of my space
or I'll cut it up for you.

I said to Widow,
Serena told me I was her charm.
She said I had a glow.

Widow said,
that glow is just you going neon on contraband,
and if you were Serena's charm
where is she now?

I said, Serena will be back.
She wouldn't go without telling me.
Serena taught me the ropes.

Yeah, Widow said, the ones we hang ourselves with.
Widow said, you think Serena is missing gone
but I say she got a date with Mr. P
and she's dead gone.

She said, who's gonna be next?
Someone's gonna lose the lottery again any day now.

But then Widow got a date and she said to me
before she drove away,
stay off my tar,

and then a car stopped for me.

Shall I to him make known as yet
my change . . . ?

Call says it's just business
and I thought, just business
while the date was breathing hard
and all the breath was pressed out of me.
I thought, just business
while he was sweating hot
and I was cold,
and I was hot
and I was cold
and while his heart beat fast and mine was still.
I was surprised he didn't sink through me
I was so nothing.

After, when I took his money,
he said,
you look innocent, like a real girl,
but you are a monster.

Standing at my corner again
and starting to yawn and sneeze and yawn
because of a lack of candy,
standing there, I thought, if I saw an angel
maybe that would mean I was a real girl
and not a monster.

Next date said,
how'd a sweet girl like you
end up in a gig like this?

I started to tell him about my shoe collection
and how it all started with that green patent Mary Jane
on the display shelf
but he said shut up.

And while the armrest was wrenching my neck
and he was breathing his sushi breath into my mouth,
while he was squeezing and pinching
and pushing his fingers into secret places,
I had to feel it without candy,
had to feel him and feel my stomach aching
and my shoulders aching
and my hips aching
and my stomach juice burning
and my eyeball juice fizzing—
that's what you get when you make a vow
about no more candy.

Next date asked, how old are you?
and I said thirteen.
I don't remember the first few birthdays
so in a way I wasn't lying,
which the street preacher says is in God's top ten.

He asked,
is this your first time?
I said yes
which in a way again I wasn't lying
because I am a pleasure virgin,
and not even with Call.

Everything was quiet
because my date had earbuds in his ears—
I couldn't hear his music
but I could hear the pain in my brain like a drum—
dopesick dopesick—
and I knew I was just getting started.

Then it was over and he asked, are you okay?
He couldn't hear my answer
but he didn't ask again
because he knew what the answer needed to be.

Little old Fred came in his little old truck,
almost a toy truck it was so small,
and the back part was wooden with no paint.
Fred's truck was a toy that got left out in the rain
and played with hard,
dents and scrapes all over,
same as Fred.

He saves up for me once a week,
wears cologne and a tie,
speaks nice to me.
He is wifeless, childless, jobless,
less, less, less.
He always gets teary that I would really take his money.

This time as he drove me back to the kiddie corner
I saw him try to steal his own money,
his little old hand in my purse.
He saw me see, and pulled out his hand
as he pulled up to my corner.
I thought, what would Serena do?

So I said, wait, I meant to give this to you,
and I handed him his money.

I said, this is Call's money.
I can't do this again.
He cried and took the money
and I said goodbye.

Widow saw me do it.

She said, why?

I said, angels.

She said, ya there's angels all right,
and every time a loony-tune chick acts stupid
one loses its wings.

I said, sometimes you have to walk a mile
in a person's shoes.

Widow said, ya and then you're a whole mile away
if you decide to keep them.
She said, what you did to get that money,
what would angels think of that?

I said, oh. That.

Next date,
he kept saying sorry sorry
because his hands sweat so bad.
He can't get a girlfriend because his hands are always slimy.

I thought, sweaty hands don't mean much
to a girl who's dopesick.
I pretended he was an alien sliming me
and the safety of all the earth
depended on me befriending him
and I would unite our planets.

Before we broke I kissed his palm.

He said, you are an angel, and gave me a big tip
and he didn't even know my name.

I told Widow with yawns and sneezes
and the water in my brain running out my eyes.

She said, hey, are you sick?

And that's when I got John the john.

John the john is a university professor.
He has told me about his mother
and his first wife
and his last girlfriend—
he says, I can't figure out women,
and looks at me as if I know something.
He says, tell me the truth, Angel—
whose fault was my divorce?
whose fault was it really?

He never touches me, only wants me to read to him
paradise lost by John Milton,
has me read book nine out of twelve
while he does his professor business.

It is about when the serpent guy
gets Eve to eat the knowledge fruit
and then everything is bad after that
and it's all her fault,
everything bad in the world is her fault
and she deserves it.

Every time Eve goes to eat that fruit,
I say in my mind, don't do it! it's a trick!

That's the only part I understand.

John told me his copy of paradise lost
is a 1935 edition.
He gives me a handwipe before I touch it.
John gets mad if I don't read it right,
makes me read it again
with a colon in my voice, not a comma,
says, don't read that like a run-on sentence you
have to put the punctuation in you don't, read
commas where there aren't any.
He said, Milton made his daughters read to him
in Latin and Greek and they didn't understand a word.
If they could do it, you can.

John said, in Milton's day punctuation was called pointing
because it pointed to the meaning.
John taught me that a semicolon is a longer pause
than a comma;
and a colon is a longer pause
than a semicolon;
and a period is the longest pause of all.
The punctuation is in English
but the rest of the book sounds foreign.

John said, Milton liked to mix up nouns and adjectives . . .
we would say, pretty young girl,
but Milton would say, pretty girl and young.

I said, oh.

He said, is that all you have to say?

I said, oh terrific that is.

John said, terrific?
You wouldn't have that word without Milton.
He made that word up.

I said, you can make words up?

He said, Milton added 630 words to our vocabulary.
Before Milton there was no
fragrance
or lovelorn,
no debauchery
or stunning,
no unprincipled.

I said,
you can make words up?

He said, some of the words didn't catch on,
like opinionastrous, meaning opinionated . . .

I said, you can make words up?

He said, book nine.

So I read
Friendly to man, far from deceit or guile.
What fear I then, rather what know to fear
Under this ignorance of good and evil . . .

I read and read.
And John liked it so much
with him doing so much hard breathing
except when I did it wrong,
which is easy when you don't get it,
when they're just words stacked up,
words like dismissive
and didactic and complacency,
all words made up by Milton,
words one after another
with commas and periods
and adjectives and verbs
all not making any sense added up.

But then none of my dates made sense,
and none of them paid as good as John.

Widow saw how much money he gave me.
I said, I have enough now to make Call happy.
Good night, Widow, have an evening good.
She rolled her eyes and said,
that John dude is one sick puppy what he's doing to you.

I said, don't forget you so beautiful look
and I left to meet Call at Kayos.

As I walked my feet beat dopesick dopesick
and my hip joints ground bone on bone
and my lips stung
and I felt like my eyeballs had rolled back into my brain.
I could see my brain thinking
you can't leave,
you think you can go home
but this is your life now,
this is what you are and what you've done.

Eyeballs can't blink back there.
They had to see that I got myself here
that I didn't care bit by bit.

On Call's candy the universe seems a friendly place,
but without it, it shows you its grumpy side.
It doesn't like you to have opinions or too many shoes.
It frowns at you
and shows you how stupid you've been.

I got to Kayos same time as Asia and his new girl—
he wasn't letting this one out of his sight—
and Call and the other businessmen were eating
and a big hot fire was burning in the firepit.
Call and the others had barbecue pork ribs,
the juice running down their chins,
and Asia's new girl laughed like Serena never was.

I didn't have the special.
In honour of Serena
who nobody was talking about
I ordered angel food cake
which they did not have but I wasn't hungry anyway.

I said to Asia's new girl, I think Serena will be back soon.
Serena was my friend. Everybody loved Serena.

Asia's girl frowned at me.

Call said, I have an idea.
I've talked to some people,
important people.

He said, the missing women,
they're getting press now
and we could cash in on that,
make it work for us,
tell people we have a way
to get them off the streets.
I mean, we could go legit, have a store.

Asia laughed, but Call said,
I've been looking into the process ...
he said, I have backers with cash.
They are offering money to pay for a lawyer.
We would have to lobby for decriminalization.

Asia said, what are you talking about, man?

Call said, I mean we could organize ourselves,
work together to get the business legalized.
Then we could set up shop anywhere, advertise on TV—
we'd be entrepreneurs.
We'd be dignified.

Asia said, with all the others watching, silent,
they'll never go for that.

Call said, wiping his red mouth,
this is a seven billion dollar business,
they can't ignore us.
What we do, it is a necessary service.
We gotta clean up our act, bind together like brothers.
Call said, it's a matter of supply and demand.

He explained how he would draw up a petition,
the men could all go out on the street to get signatures
and take them to town hall and the mayor.

Asia said, you do it, Call baby.
You do it. We're behind you.

I thought, the missing women getting press?
what did that mean?
what did the press care if they were just running away
or checking into rehab or going to jail?
I thought, what if Widow was right?
what if Serena was dead gone, not missing gone?
what if there was a Mr. P?

While Call and Asia and the other businessmen laughed
and ate their barbecue pork ribs
I tried to imagine being dead,
and what if it was no feeling, no dreaming, no nothing,
just not existing?

I closed my eyes, and what if she got suffocated?
I held my breath until I couldn't stand it,
but she would have had to stand it
all the way to being dead.

I had to stop because dying is not a thing you can do
with your imagination.

When I opened my eyes Asia and his new girl
were looking at me, and I said again,
Serena will be back soon.

Asia said, what's wrong with her?

Call said, we have to go,
she skipped a dose,
she's bringing the mood down.
I'll call you about the petition.

Walking back to his place I said to Call,
the press says about the missing girls?
Widow says there's a Mr. P—
what if he got Serena?

Call said, Mr. P—that's just street talk.
Cops say one person could not get away with it that long,
that many girls, all those bodies.
What could he be doing with all those bodies?
Call said, you see the police every night driving around,
you see their cars and them inside.
Have you ever seen Mr. P?
He said, but anyway, it will get people to sign my petition.

Call believes in the police—
they are clean and pressed in their uniforms
and polished boots
and firearms and badges
and pins.
Call is respectful of them, jokes with them on the streets.

But I thought,
would Serena go away without telling me?
would she leave without her running-away money
which is still under my mattress?

At his place, Call said, you just need a little candy,
that's what this is all about.
I said, no thank you

and he said, what's going on?
you getting ideas?

I said, you have to be pure
if you want to see an angel.

He laughed, said, pure?

I nodded
and my brain went slosh slosh
and the juice in my eyeballs fizzed.

Call sat on the broken-bone couch
like nothing was wrong with it,
tipped sideways on it like he was straight
and all the rest of the world was crooked,
and he wrote something and said it was a letter
and he made me sit beside him and read his letter.

Dear Mayor.

Every year our municipality, spends valuable tax dollars, monitoring the activities of sex trade perpetrators. Every year hundreds of young women, are killed because of violence; many more: die of disease and drug related health problems.

Imagine a world: where this service was legalized; where women were required to go for regular medical checkups: this would make patrons much safer. I propose: a community where these activities are contained; and where everyone benefits from the millions of dollars of tax revenue that could be reaped from this industry.

We are starting a petition and would like to arrange an appointment to meet with you, to discuss some of our lobby group's ideas for change.

Sincerely,
C. B. Jones,
Entrepreneur
Cell 604-555-0199

Call was impressed with all his extra commas
and colons and semicolons.
He said, what do you think, Angel?

I said, opinionastrous.

Call said, someday we'll have a duplex and a dog
and cut the grass in the evening
and invite the neighbours to a barbecue.
He said, you make enough money,
and we'll be folks, we'll have a baby.

He picked up a magazine and showed me the ads
telling people to spray perfume on furniture
and adopt a manatee
and cook with balsamic vinegar and toasted hazelnuts
and thyme sprigs and goat cheese.
He said, this will be us someday.

But all those ingredients were just a poem to me.

He said, time to expand the business.

Me first he ruined ... whom will he next?

Tonight started out with the same dialogue,
with Widow saying,
you again?
She said, I'm nobody's babysitter
fine by me you wanna get dead
see if I care.
She said, you watch out
don't you be thinking I'll save you
and don't you get in that car there either
I heard he's a woman-hater.
She said, don't step over that line.

She said, what's the matter with you? you dopesick?
Call cut you off? why then?
you want to feel it the way you did the first time? why then?
how can you stand it?
don't you throw up around me,
throwup makes me throw up.

She said, how can you work?

I said, when I'm clean I'll find out your real name,
and she said, guess.

I said, is it Marnie?
Lenora?
Dorothy?
Elaine?

Widow listened to each name,
trying it on,

and
no
no
no
no.

I said, Widow is a nice name
and she said, too spidery.

I said, call your mom.
She said, I don't remember my mom.
She said, some date knocked my memories out of me
but I bet if I hear my real name
I'll know.
If I could remember my name
I might remember my mom who gave it to me.

Then came Mr. Mercedes pointing at me
and Mr. Shiny Suburban who pinched
and the guy who had his girlfriend on his cell all the while
and the guy who had a Mickey Mouse watch
and Mickey danced the whole time
and the guy who asked me for a password
and was sure I was a spy
and the nice man whose girl was far away.

The whole time I was shaking and sweating and coughing
and one man said stop it
but no matter how hard I tried I couldn't stop
shaking and coughing and yawning.
He put his hand over my mouth
until he was done
so I could hardly breathe—
and right then and there I gave up.

I said, Widow, I'm done.

I walked back to Call's place same as always
knowing he would give me give me give me
all the candy I could take.

I walked back to Call's place
thinking, I give up,
thinking, I'm dying I'm dying,
and me not knowing,
just walking in the door,
and there I found

an angel.

A little one.

A little girl.

Call said, you needed some help.

He said, her name is Melli.

His words replete with guile into her heart
too easy entrance won...

Melli, a little girl
you could see her veins through
and her eyelids?
you could see the blue through
and her feet?
you could see the bones through
and her hair?
you could see the light through

She was almost not there.

I thought, if I blink
I could make her go away—
but no
she was never gone, blink blink,
she was there and there
and what was I going to do?

The air of this place
could crush such bones
                such blue.

I said, where did you get her?
He said, group home here,
nobody cares about those kids.

I said, that's not true—
I said, I'll work hard—
I said, take her back
it's not right
she's too little—
I said, if you got caught you would be in big trouble.

Call said, all great businessmen take risks.
I said please.

He said, you need some candy,
and I said, just a minute.

I had to think, had to,
but I knew I couldn't think on Call's candy.

I said, in a minute.

I threw up in Call's bathroom sink
so hard I thought bits of stomach
slid out of my mouth
and then I came back into Call's living room.

Melli.

I was careful, didn't move too fast around her,
didn't want to scare her.

Call said, I need to go out,
and he went into the bathroom
and ran the shower, started singing
something about little miss strange
no one knows where she comes from—

While Call sang in the shower,
I asked her, how old are you?

She put up all ten fingers
and then one—
same age as my little brother Jeremy.

It's okay, I said to her, my voice shaking, shaking,
you can trust me—
what's group home?
where are your parents?

But my words went through her
as if she weren't solid
and she didn't answer.

I said, Melli, is that your real name?
She nodded.
I said, can you talk?
She shrugged, looked down.

Why don't you talk?
I looked in her mouth,
she let me,
and she had a tongue
pink as a baby's
and I knew that mouth
had never eaten fruit off the knowledge tree.

I said, it's okay, silent Melli—
it's okay.

I said, Melli, where are you from?
where do you live?

I looked in the phone book,
but Group Connect
        Group Sales Office
        Group Telecom
        Grout
        Grove
no Group Home.

I said, Melli, where is Group Home?
What is it near?
She looked away, looked around,
looked sad that she didn't know the answers to the quiz.

I said, what's your last name?
I said, do you write, Melli? write your last name,
and I gave her paper and she printed neatly
Smith.

Sometimes God thinks he is so funny.

Call came in holding out candy,
offered it to Melli,
said, wanna try?
I said, she's too young,
and he said, mind your own business.
But he left her alone anyway.

I held Melli's hand and took her in the bedroom
and I whispered,
don't, 'kay?
Trust me, Melli,
sometimes one bite
and everything's different after that.

I put her to bed,
tucked the blanket under her chin
like I used to with Jeremy
and I lay beside her on top of the blanket
and didn't stare at her until she was asleep.

Getting a little girl makes you stop pretending,
makes you remember things,
makes you sick
makes you see
makes you say
this is what happened to me . . .

When I wished for an angel
this isn't what I meant at all.

She's just a little girl.

I caught Call looking at me
looking at her sleeping,
and he knew I was thinking, just you touch her,
just you touch her.

I said, quiet, so I didn't wake her up,
you don't have to put her to work,
I'll make lots of money.

Call said, this is just business,
right, Angel?
Someday I'll be legal,
someday the government will acknowledge
this is just business
and give me a license
and I'll pay my taxes like any other guy.
He said, I'll be a marketing guy, a retail man . . .

I saw me and Melli, mannequins in his store window,
mute and hard, undressed,
but still wearing our shoes,
still wearing our smiles.

He said, you want your sweet candy now?

And I said, no thank you.

I used to be afraid that Call didn't love me
but now I knew I didn't love him.

Call said,
she's in for a million.
You be her main girl, Angel.

That's what he said.

He said, you be the boss of her.

I said, I would never,
and he said, you'll do what I say,
and I said, I'll die first,
and he said, okay.

And then he showed me pictures,
pictures of Jeremy
at the playground
sliding
swinging
hanging
testing gravity
pretending to die.

Call said, I visited Jeremy a few weeks ago.
I walked him home from the playground
to keep him safe.
He said, he's cute, huh?
and my heart was
sliding
swinging
hanging
and I saw the gravity
of the situation.

I laughed and said, what a brat,
I ripped up the pictures one by one
until just a Jeremy eye
and a Jeremy mouth
all in pieces on the floor.

I don't care, I said, I don't care.
But Call was smiling
and I was dying for real.

Then he showed me a stuffed blue rhino.

I had seen that stuffed blue rhino before.
I had bought this very stuffed rhino
and given it to Jeremy.

I took it from Call, smelled it, smelled Jeremy on it,
grass and jam and sour milk,
and my brain shook, I felt it rattle in my skull,
right behind my nose
like my brain came loose,
picked right off the stem.

Call said, if you leave me, if you take Melli,
I'll hurt Jeremy.
Nothing bad will happen to Jeremy
as long as you remember that.
I said, why would you say something like that?
and he hit me
and that was the right answer.

Call went out
and I slept on top of the blanket beside Melli
and I dreamed
that Call stretched and shrank,
stretched and shrank in his skin—
I never knew what he would be next—
a whale? a gnat? a wolf? a sea bird?
a snake . . . ?
every one could swallow me whole,
that's how small I was.

I dreamed that it was all a dream . . .

But when I woke up she was still there.

Hate stronger, under show of love
well feigned . . .

She was lying silent beside me,
staring at me, not moving,
and it was people's lunchtime
so I said, you must be hungry.

I got up and in the bathroom threw up
maybe bits of spleen
and my shoulders ached like the time Call beat me
because I said I was too tired to work.
It was like my back and shoulders
remembered everything.
But Melli had to eat.

Call said,
now it's my turn to stand on the corner,
collect names for my petition.

I said, take your time.
Good luck.
Goodbye.

He said, take care of her,
she's your retirement plan.
She's here so you can be the baby mom,
have my baby someday.
So take care of her.

I said, yes I will, and I did not lie,
top ten.

And he locked us in.

I looked in the kitchen and found

pasta
white bread
salt
instant potatoes
vanilla ice cream
milk
cottage cheese
cauliflower
plain yogurt
bananas
cream of wheat
mayonnaise
mozzarella
and sponge cake.

I said, Melli, are you hungry?
I gave her a mozzarella cheese sandwich
with mayonnaise
and milk to drink
but I couldn't eat anything.

Melli sat on the broken-bone couch in a ball
silent, silent—whatever I said to her
she didn't answer.

I said, Melli, when you're a kid
you think if you break the rules
you will die.

But one day you break the rules, and you don't die,
and then you think you'll never die.
You dump all the rules and you're so light you float.

But you can get so high
there's no air up there.
You can get so high there's nothing to see but clouds
that rain you down.

Don't, 'kay?
Don't take Call's candy, 'kay?

I said, who runs Group Home?
what's her name? do you remember a name?
but she just shrugged, shook her head.

I said, what's your daddy's name?
Write your daddy's name,
and she wrote Mike.
The phone book had lots of Mike and Michael Smiths
but none of them were the dad of Melli.
No one was the dad, brother or uncle of a Melli.

After a while I started not understanding the word no.
It sounded strange to me.

Michael Smith number I don't know said no,
and I said yes?
He said no,
and I said what?
He said, what part of no don't you understand?

I said, the first part
and the last part.

I said, Melli, what about your mom?
Write your mom's name—
so she wrote Sue neat and careful
and the phone book had lots
of Sue Smiths too.

I called every S, Sue, and Susan Smith
and none of them had misplaced a little girl.

But Suzanna Smith had a dog named Melli,
named after a distant cousin—
she hadn't seen that cousin in twenty-three years
which made Suzanna cry.

Melli lay on the couch
and looked at me
and didn't care that a dog had her name.

I said to Melli, time to listen up.
All the little children in the world aren't lucky
and Melli, you are one of the unluckies.
I'm sorry, but it is so.
I'm sorry to tell you that
but you have to help me, Melli.
I'm not feeling so good.

But Melli was silent, silent.

I thought, what am I going to do?
what am I going to do?

Right then Call came back.
He said, I've been trying to call,
he said, no more phone privileges,
and he smashed me into the wall
and Melli started to cry.
I said, don't be sad, Melli, don't cry.
It doesn't hurt ...
Call said, ripping the phone jack out,
from now on I'll use my cell.

Later I whispered to Melli,
ha ha things on me that have been broken
by Call and by dates:

nose,
finger,
toe,
eardrum.

But angels don't break, Melli, I said.
Angels are bendy.
Ha ha, Melli. Ha ha, right?
Don't cry, 'kay?

Call said later, I forgive you,
said, here's your candy.
But I said no and not even no thank you just no.
He said, you'll come begging for it
I'll make you beg, you know that—
and don't think about getting it somewhere else,
they all know you're mine
and I've put the word out.

He said, get out there,
we'll see if you can do your job without it—
no skin off my nose.

But it is, I can tell it scares him.
And me.

He said, get out there
and take her with you.
You don't want her to work, fine,
but you make double.

So I held Melli's hand as we walked
to the gate of ten thousand happinesses
and I said, sorry, sorry, but it's better you are with me
than alone with Call.

She patted my back when I coughed
and didn't mind when I yawned and yawned at her.
I said, Melli, even my fingertips are sick
even my toes are sick
even my hair is sick.

On the way to my corner
we stopped at the Carnegie library
and I wrote a note for the message board
with my hands shaking from lack of candy

> *Dear owner of Melli Smith,*
> *I know where your little girl is.*
> *Please leave your phone number.*
> *You have done a very good job with her.*
> *Angel*

I folded it and pinned it to the message board.
On the outside I wrote,
Looking for Melli?

I thought,
this is the kind of plan you get
when you don't do candy even if you are sick,
and I thought, stained-glass Milton would be proud.

Widow said, not you again
I'm nobody's babysitter.
What the——!

She said, get that baby home to its mama.
She said, where did you get it?

I said, Call. He says finders keepers.

Widow saw how it was.
She stared at Melli, no blinking,
until tears came out.

I said, don't cry Widow,
I'm going to return her as soon as I get a good plan.
I wrote a letter to my dad.
When he comes to get me
he'll take Melli too.

Widow said, who's crying?
She said, tell her about the line.

Widow said, looks like Call got himself a twinkie,
sweet and soft, all cream on the inside—

Widow said, that's how you started out,
wrapped and fresh, iced for the kiddie stroll—
but everybody eats twinkies up
and throws the wrapper in the garbage
and nobody cares
and that's what you get
for being a twinkie.

She said, I might have been a twinkie once
but I don't remember.

I stood at my corner
and Melli in the shadows
and me in my yellow tutu
and mismatched shoes,
but tonight even my shoes couldn't make me feel better.

My shoes said,
what are you doing here?
what are you waiting for?

And I said, shut up.
I have to make up for Melli.

I said,
Widow, I gotta make double tonight.
Call said.

She said, maybe thinking angels will help.

And I said, maybe,
and she snorted.

So I said, angel, angel,
just like Serena said to do,

and just then a car pulled up.

In it was twins, two little men dressed the same,
and one said, we pay double,
and Widow's mouth fell open.
I said to her, will you watch Melli?
and she didn't say no.

When I got back
Widow said, you just got lucky,
just luck.

I threw up on the sidewalk, all white.

She said, gack, lucky you did that
on your side of the line.

Then the man who had dirty hair
and the teenage boy who was scared
and the man who thought halfway through
I was somebody he knew from Seattle
and he called her name over and over
and the man who never said a word
but hated with his eyes
and the man who told me what his suit cost
and his watch cost
and said, you're burning up, I like it that way—

and every time I came back Melli was okay.

Without candy
I saw how every time
I was only in the man's wishes, not a real girl,
just a guess, a question, a story he made up—

but every time I got out of a car
Melli was in the good hiding dark,
clean and smelling of wind and rain,
and she was real, a real girl,
and not even a story I made up.

After the man in the expensive suit,
Widow said, take this baby home,
you're too sick to work.
She said, I'll give you all my cash if you can guess my name.

So I said,
    Ruby?
    Elsie?
    Yvonne?
    Sharon?
    Tania?

Widow bit down on each one
and said,
    no
    no
    no
    no
    no.

She said, here's my cash anyway
just for trying
and don't think I'll ever do this again.

I thought of Serena's money under my mattress,
but I couldn't use it because what if she came for it?
So I said, thanks Widow.

She pointed to the line
and my toe which she owned.

I said thank you and took her hard-work money
and that gave me more shame
than all the money I took from men.

On the way back to Call's place,
holding Melli's hand
we passed where Sarah wasn't there anymore
and she wrote poems and drew unicorns crying always crying.
We passed where Janet wasn't there anymore
and she was a member of a champion softball team.
They both liked things
before they came to Hastings and Main.

Now they were missing
like Serena,
and they never came back.

My bones creaked while I thought,
Serena . . .
bone on bone,
while my stomach folded up
and all the shiny, slimy stuff
that should have been in my brain
was running out of my face—

but I knew then, I knew then
that Widow was right.
Serena wasn't coming back.

Melli and I came in
and I gave the money to Call
shaking, my whole body shaking and aching.

I threw up again so hard
I thought I threw up a bit of liver,
a piece of me sliding invisible
out of my mouth
and down the drain.

Call said, you want your candy now?
and I said, in a minute,
but I thought, no no no not yet.

I drank some water
and threw it up with what felt like a piece of lung
and I drank some more
and rinsed my face
and brushed my teeth
and why didn't Serena's body wash up on shore?
why didn't joggers find her bones in the woods?
why didn't garbagemen find her in a dumpster
all red with blood and ketchup?

I knew why now.

It was because our girls
all went to the same place to die—
the secret place,

they dropped down to the underplace,
with bones and worms and rot—

Serena was dead.

I lay down on the bed
and I said, Melli, Serena is dead.

She didn't answer. Surprise.

I said, they never come back,
somebody should tell the police they never come back.

Melli didn't answer.

I said, you think someone is going to save you?
my voice shaking the snot out of me,
you think if you just sit there all big blue eyes
and blue tears coming out
not swearing, not stealing,
keeping the commandments like jewels in a box
like they're made of gold
you think an angel is going to save you?
you think that?

And then I hugged her and said,
don't be sad, Melli, don't be sad, don't—

I told her about Serena
and how she said, friend, you are welcome
for hot dogs and church.

I said,
Serena—I bet she's serene now.
I bet she's not hungry in heaven.
I bet God gave her a good address:
Cloud Nine, even.

The worst thing was
Serena ending up being stolen
by someone else's story—
just a character in his story,
and the ending she wanted to have
got him instead,
just a part of his stupid story . . .
that was the worst thing of all.

I threw up again,
maybe with a chunk of heart,
and Call came in and I said,
do you see any bits of heart in there?
He said, you're losing it,
said, this could all be over in a minute
if you take your candy,
and I forgot to answer because I was thinking,

he can't have her anymore,
I'm writing a new end to her story,
I'm taking Serena's story back.

I lay by Melli, yawning, yawning, and my legs jumping,
trying to be still and not cough or shake.
I whispered, Dad must have my letter by now
and what if he came for us?
Because I knew a girl whose family did that—

I didn't tell Melli
that when that girl got home people looked at her
like they look at people whose faces have been burned off,
whose faces have melted,
people looked at her like they wondered
why she would want to live—
so she came back to Hastings and Main.

But what will not ambition and revenge
descend to?

Melli and I woke up
and I made breakfast for her,
cream of wheat, which I ate a little.

Call was stroking the pages of names on his petition
signed by people who want us off the streets,
people who worry about their children.

He said, see, Angel?
I can do this.

He said some of the names out loud,
read them like poetry,
admired their curly t's and y's,
did not fold the pages.

He was in a good mood
like the Call I met at the mall
like the one who gave me my first kiss
so I said,
Call, maybe there are angels.

He ran his fingers down the list of names
and didn't answer, so I said,
maybe we should take Melli back
because of possible angels,
because an angel would mean God
and he would want us to give Melli back.

Call said, you are crazy dopesick.

He sat on the broken-bone couch
trying to be patient with me.

He said, you think there's God?
You think when you die you go to a good place?
You get to meet the head universe maker?

Get real, he said, get real.

He said, God is a crutch.
He said, religion causes all the wars.

I said, what religion was Hitler?

He said, I can't have a conversation with you.
God is an imaginary friend for grownups.

People like you will believe anything, Call said.

I bet you believe people went to the moon.
But that was a trick to explain
what they did with all that money.
Look at the footage, he said—the flag is waving . . .
What's wrong with that picture, Angel?
No air, that's what. There's no air on the moon
for a flag to wave in.

He said, I'm glad we had this talk.

Then Asia came over to see Call's name collection
and show him his.
I did not understand what they were talking about,
something trying to get backing
from a member of the taxation committee,
something imposing an entertainment tax
in exchange for movement toward regulation,
something the right to advertise the product
which would normalize the business.
They could give complimentary services to legislators . . .

They started laughing together
and Call shouted at me,
Supply! you're in demand.

I said, Melli and me, can we go for milk and bread?
And he said, hey it's okay between us, right, Angel?
I can trust you, right?
He plumped up Jeremy's rhino,
said, I know you're my girl,
buy me some ham while you're there,
said, why don't you stop by the library.

Which was weird.

We walked downstairs
and I held Melli's hand because I wobbled
and I explained to Melli with coughs
and my face on fire
and my hips out of joint
about why I couldn't run away.

I said, if I leave, Call will hurt my brother Jeremy.
And if I saw Jeremy in heaven
I would be so sorry,
I would say, it was all my fault.
Melli, I would die of Jeremy
if anything happened to him.
But there's that letter to my dad,
in which I told him about Serena and my vow.

I checked the mailbox,
but nothing.

Not yet, Melli, I said.
Just not yet.
But soon.

In the window of the store where we bought milk
we saw a missing children's poster,
each little child in her own square
as herself and as the computer aged her
and with new computer hair.
Melli's picture wasn't on it.
Neither was mine. None of the faces were mine.

I wondered how those kids felt,
stars of the missing children's poster club,
but not being anywhere, just missing.
I wondered if they ever said,
I would never wear my hair like that.

After we bought milk and white bread
and tomatoes because Call is allergic,
I took Melli on the coal harbour walk.
Showed her my favourite gingerbread houseboat
and told her about how I dreamed of floating it out to sea
and how I would have kelp for my garden
and waves for my winter.

I showed her how to feed the pigeons
with our bread,
and they let her touch them,
let her stroke their necks
shiny as purple-glitter nail polish.

The pigeons never let anyone touch them...

It's a wing thing, I guess.

She held my hand while we walked,
held me up,
and I didn't throw up once.

In a vacant lot
some people were making
a pop-up storybook park
all out of throwaways
and scraps and string,
all out of finders keepers
and losers weepers,
out of duct tape and rags,
cartons and castoffs . . .

Melli and I looked at it through the fence.

On the way back
we stopped at the library
and I showed her Mr. Milton
in stained glass.

I checked the message board without belief
but then I almost screamed
because there was the note
with my name on it!

I opened it, shaking,
and it said,

Nice try.
Call

When we got back
Call said, did you stop by the library?
I said, no I never go there.

He laughed and held up his candy
and said, this is going to be a long day for you
without candy,
said, get ready for work.
I said, it's not time yet,
I have to sleep,
and he said, get ready.

Before you do the streets today
I need you to be nice to one of my backers,
one of my money men, at his place of business.
He said, you think I like this?
all you think about is you,
you never think about what this is doing to me ...

He said, Angel, do you love me?
Just do this for me, for us—
soon we'll be taxpayers,
we'll have the neighbours over, we'll volunteer.
You with me, baby?

I got up to go because he wasn't really asking,
and Call locked Melli in
and I found out Call's backer was a baby dentist
with goldfish in his wall
and little couches for kids to sit in.

Call said, I don't care how sick you are,
you smile and be sweet
or I'll stuff that candy down your throat.

The baby dentist put me in that chair
that turned me almost upside down
and said, is this your first time?
Don't be scared,
I'm just going to have a little look,
just open your mouth like an O
and say ahhh . . .
He didn't even have to give me freezing
because I was already numb.

While he did his backer business
I thought about Serena,
wondering if she danced in heaven
and if God said, may I?
and spun her a galaxy,
and if he said, haven't I always taken care of you?
and she said no
and he said sorry.

I thought about something I heard
about a skydiver whose parachute didn't open
but he lived.
He remembered hitting the ground
like it was all pillows
because the unconscious part
came before the hurting part.

Maybe it was that way for Serena . . .
it would be just like God to do it that way.

In a dentist chair
when you're so upside down
and you don't have anything else to hang on to
you want to believe maybe this isn't all you get—
when so many people try to beat the angel out of you,
you hang on for dear life.

And then the baby dentist was done
and I lived.
I always live.

When I got home
Melli was playing solitaire—
she smiled when we came in and I said,
Call, Melli has such nice teeth,
good thing she'll never have to go to the baby dentist.

He knew what I meant
and he knew how much I meant it.
He said, I'm going out,
and he locked us in.

I got my notebook
and figured out
when you start to write a poem
you don't know where it might go.
It's an act of faith to write a book of you,
to believe a poem
is something you could do.

When you write a poem
you get to be a baby god-girl
and in you is a tiny universe, a dollhouse universe
with planets the size of peas and suns like marbles
all inside you . . .

and if you write it good enough
you could maybe spin the world backwards—
maybe I could watch myself walking backwards
walking away from Call and all the men
and putting the shoes back on the display shelf
and walking backwards until I was a dot
and disappeared.

I watched Melli play solitaire a long time
and she always lost
and she always started again.

When Call came back
he found me in the bathroom,
staring into the toilet
wondering if my appendix was floating in there.

He said, you can't work that way,
and I thought, yes that is true,
but I said, it's better for business
don't you see?
the clients like it better
when you're not numb—
they like it better when you can feel everything.

He smiled, said, that's my girl.
Get out there and do good business.
Don't mess things up for me now, okay Angel?
Not now, okay?
Just think about me for once.
And remember, you're working for two.
I can't keep feeding her for nothing.

So Melli and I
went out again where the girls are hungry
while they hunt,
prowling, silent, looking for Mr. Steak Dinner,
Mr. Baked Potato and Butter,
where the girls say, all nice as can be,
I'll have mine rare
just a little blood in the middle—
they lick the bones, suck out the marrow.
They can't waste any of it.
It's always cold at night by the sea.

My intended wing depressed . . .

At the gate of ten thousand happinesses
Widow was already there
smoking and spitting
all dressed in black
hard as pavement,
and she said,
oh lord, get me some diapers,
this place is turning into some kinda day care—
said, I thought it was a bad high,
but you two keep turning up,
said, one of these days
I'm gonna collect that toe.

Widow said, there's the Preacher,
he's here for me.
But he pulled up and pointed at me.

Widow said, he's a midtrack guy,
he means me,
and she walked to his car.

But he pointed at me again.

So I went, said, watch Melli for me.
Widow scowled at him as we drove away,
at me, too,
and I was scared with no candy
and so far no angel around a corner
and me knowing now about Mr. P
and Serena being dead.

Maybe Preacher was Mr. P,
and what if this car was crowded with ghosts—
crammed in the back,
one in the rear window,
one pushing the gas pedal,
nodding their loose heads,
laughing through slashed-open throats,
holding their gashed bellies—

I couldn't help it,
while he was doing his business
I whispered,

angel, angel,
and he said, shut up.

So I shut up while he dirtied me down,
and I kept thinking, got to get enough for two,
enough to cover for Melli.

Without candy I saw
when afterwards his face was disgusted,
when his face said, why do I do this? I can't stand myself
and I can't stand you . . . that's what I saw on his face
without candy.

When he brought me back he said, you're so skinny,
I shouldn't have to pay the full amount.
So he only gave me half.
I was so happy to have no knives poking in me
I didn't even say thief.

Melli was still okay.

Drive-by eyes couldn't get enough of us.
They stared like bullets, broke their necks to see us.
Some spat at us as they drove by.
Everybody laughed.
We are so funny.

I said, Melli, don't be sad. Be sad for them.
They break their soul bones to touch us.

I got picked up again and again
and Melli kept being okay when I got back.

Widow said, you're going to have to pay me for babysitting
and it better be good.

Next a man who told me he was eighty
and I said, you must be so proud.

Then a man who was a child psychologist,
and I said, you must enjoy your research.

Then a man who brought his baby girl asleep in the back seat
and I wouldn't have done it except still not enough for two.

After that I threw up on my side of the line
just water and bubbles.

Widow said, even when you're sick
that baby face of yours brings in the cash,
but not enough for two.
She said, free babysitting, then,
but still not enough for two.
She said, what are you going to do?
You thinking angels, right now, babyface?
Is it helping, huh?

And just then John the john pulled up.

Widow shook her head.

I said, Melli, this might take a while,
but don't you worry, he pays good.

John opened paradise lost to book nine
and gave me the wipes
before I could touch it.

I read the best I could.
But he got mad and said,
that sentence has an elliptical clause,
so read it like that. He talked about
subordinate conjunctions
and the subjunctive mood.

What fear I then? rather, what know to fear
Under this ignorance of good and evil,
Of God or death, of law or penalty?
Here grows the cure of all, this fruit divine,
Fair to the eye, inviting to the taste,
Of virtue to make wise: What hinders then
To reach, and feed at once both body and mind?
    So saying, her rash hand in evil hour
Forth reaching to the fruit, she plucked, she ate.
Earth felt the wound; and Nature from her seat
Sighing through all her works gave signs of woe,
That all was lost.

I read a long time while he breathed hard—
I wanted to keep reading,
I felt like I was getting it.
I said, how does it end?
the very last book, how does it end?

and John said, none of your business,
that is enough for tonight,
and gave me a big tip.

Almost, but still not enough for two.

Widow was on a date,
but Melli was safe, sunk into the shadows,
and she was falling asleep there on the street
for anyone to see, for anyone to take,
and I couldn't leave her again.

So I took her past the Jimi Hendrix shrine
and I took her past stained-glass Milton in the library
and I couldn't believe I was taking her back
without enough for two,
but I was.

Melli and I walked into Slingin' Ink
and Tattoo started talking about his hero Tom Leppard,
who lives on the Isle of Skye in Scotland
and has leopard skin inked on every place on his body
except between his toes and inside his ears.

He said, what do you think of that, Angel?
You can paint your body
to be whatever you want.

He said, all I want is a girl of my own
who will let me draw on her, who will be my blank canvas,
but a girl like that is hard to find.
He said, Call is lucky,
he gets to decide who you are.

Tattoo said,
you think yours is the oldest profession?
No way, mine's older.

I heard of a hunter from five thousand years ago
they found freeze-dried in a glacier
and he had tattoos—
you beat that, Angel.

And some king of England back in the middle ages
died in a big battle,
and how did they find his body on the battlefield?
His tats, that's how.
We're in ancient business, Angel.

He said, Angel—when?

I said, you can't afford me.

He said, name a price.

I said how much I needed,
so it would be enough for two.

He said, don't tell Call it was me.
He's a cadaver.
He doesn't talk at all
when I'm slinging ink.
He's not alive on his skin,
he wants evil scraped into him—
I'm telling you, Angel, they're the worst kind,
I don't want to mess with him.

I said, I won't tell,
and I pulled down my shirt collar
to show him my shoulder . . .

I could see that was driving him crazy,
him imagining my canvas.

I lay down on his table
and he carved me up,

whistling, singing his breath into my skin . . .
while Melli watched the stairs and me and the stairs,
while Tattoo talked and cut me up,

I said, Melli, it doesn't hurt,
don't worry . . . it doesn't.

So Tattoo said, fine,
I'll kick it into third,
pound some skin—

When he was done his face was disappointed
and I looked and he'd put a wing on my shoulder,
so real, so feathers,
pretty and weepy and bleeding,
but he was not proud—

He said, that's not what I wanted, not what I meant.
How did you do that? How did you make my hand go
that way? I didn't mean a wing! My mind was bent.
Whatever I want, that was the plan—I'd go slow,
I'd paint you the proof that I have a universe
in my brain, but you put a curse
on my art, and it's your fault . . .

He threw me the money
and I went upstairs, slow, with Melli in tow
and enough for two.

When I gave the money to Call
he was in a good mood
because of getting twice as much
and still having Melli in the bank . . .

but then he saw blood on my shirt
and he looked
and he punched my wing
until it wasn't a wing anymore
just a bruise with feathers.

He said, Tattoo,
and I said, no
and he said, ya it was
and I said, Call, it was all my fault,
and he said, don't think you won't pay.

He went downstairs to spill Tattoo's ink,
and I heard something fall, and,
not my gun!
not my needles! and Call laughing—
I heard pounding, Call having fun
wrecking everything
and Tattoo crying
and Call saying, if you go to the cops about this . . .

Melli and I curled up in bed together
and this time Melli stroked my hair
and I said, if Call kills us
maybe we will be angels
light enough to fly in the clouds and sleep on them.
We will have white hair
and wear bride dresses every day
and walk through walls if we want
and watch movies for free.

Then Call came upstairs
and I waited for him to be mad at me still.

But he just stood looking at me,
said, I'm going to forgive you in good faith.
I'm not a bad guy, Angel,
you know that—
I'm just trying to do good business,
good business is good for everybody,
are you hearing me, Angel?
But, baby, I can only be so patient,
you understand?
You have to do what I say—
if you give me problems
how will my backers believe I can expand the business?
You think I'm scary, you should see them.

Call kissed me, said, our petition, our petition,
soon things will be different.
He kissed me, said,
now whenever you go through Slingin' Ink
you'll remember to be good,
you'll remember you and Melli belong to me.

I went into the kitchen
and cut up the tomatoes.
Tomatoes are really fruits.
Nobody knows what kind of fruit
was on the tree of knowledge in book nine—
what if it was tomatoes?
People always blame apples,
but how do they know it was apples?
Maybe once tomatoes grew on trees
and after Eve they got demoted.

I cut up a tomato
and there—the shape of an angel
between the seeds like stars . . .

I cut up another and another—
there was an angel shape in every one
and I sprinkled them with sugar.

Then I ate them
and I kissed Call
in my same mouth
where I had eaten tomatoes and angels with sugar
but he didn't die.

But past who can recall, or done undo?

When I woke up
I thought, today is Sunday.
Without candy,
you know stuff like that.

Melli was already awake, playing solitaire,
never cheating, always losing.

Call was watching her, just watching,
said to me,
she never cheats.
He put the rhino on the kitchen table,
said, I've got business.
You go shopping,
buy yourself some new shoes,
two of them.
This is your chance to prove yourself, right Angel?
You be good and I don't lock you in anymore.

He went out,
and just before he did
he squeezed Jeremy's rhino around its neck.

I said, Melli, Call wants us to be good,
so let's be good.
It's Sunday.
Let's go to church.

Call had trashed Slingin' Ink to pandemonium
everything broken and holes in the walls
and lights pulled down
and no Tattoo in sight.

We waded through the needles and gloves
and spilled inks and tipped-over furniture
and rubber grips and sample books . . .
my shoulder throbbed where Call beat up my wing
but I said, we're going to church.

I was scared walking to the church,
the Church of Church Wednesdays of Hot Dogs for the Dead.

But at the church steps I heard singing and I said,
hear that, Melli? they're singing.
And instead of opening the door, I walked into it.

Melli touched my face where I bumped into the door.
I said, Melli, I thought I was so nothing
I could walk right through that door.

Wow, I said, church has already taught me
that nothing is something I never was
and never can be.

We walked in
and I walked into the chapel like a bride,
and everyone looked at us.

I walked down the aisle, my hands folded before me,
holding my invisible bouquet, and they saw me
and, what is she doing here?
They put loving arms around their children and stared,
and I put a loving arm around Melli to show I understood.

The reverends were husband and wife,
Adam and Eve in their churchy Eden.

Mrs. Reverend talked about Restitution.
She read about Restitution from her book:
"For he should make full restitution;
If he have nothing, then he shall be sold for his theft . . ."
And I thought, is that what happened to me?
for stealing display shoes?

Mr. Reverend wore a diamond in his ear,
as if his face were married to God—
his ear was saying,
I'm listening with sparkles,
I'm hearing with stars . . .

Then music as good as Jimi Hendrix
and stained glass as good as John Milton
and then to taste of sacrament hors d'oeuvres,
to eat low angel food—

and then it was over.

Mrs. Reverend came to me after and said, welcome.

I said, I liked thee poem.
She said, thank you.
I said, the angels helped thy write it.
She said, yes, maybe, I hope so.
I said, have thy ever seen an angel?
She said, sometimes you can entertain one unawares.

I said, yes, that is true.

She said, what is your name?

I said, Angel, and this is Melli, Melli Smith,
daughter of Mike and Sue Smith—
do you know them?

She shook her head and I stared at her
and she stared at me
and then all the people came to touch her hand
and hug her.

I walked away
with Melli's hand in mine,
with Restitution in mind.

Back at Call's place,
where he wasn't home yet from his business,
I opened his closet
and looked at all the shoes—
I said, Restitution, Melli.

I picked up the shoes one by one,
my gillie-tasselled boot
and my colour-block suede pump,
my alligator sabrina
and my plaid wellington,
my curve-wedge heel with rhinestones . . .

I picked them up,
held them,
said goodbye.

Sometimes you have to do drastic things,
I said out loud to Melli,
sometimes you have to choose.

I packed up all the shoes into bags,
said, Restitution,
and between one word and another
I figured out that's what believing does—
it's a shape for words to live in,
it's a pretend meaning for a little while,
and if you leave it there long enough
it hardens into something true.

If I took those shoes back,
nobody could take that away from me.

Melli and I walked to the store.
She had a bag of only ones
and I had a bag of only ones
and I picked a lucky shoe store
and we went in with our bags full of shoes.

Right away I saw the most beautiful shoe on display,
one with red patent leather uppers and
a tiny brass buckle
and on the sole it said Isabella Fiore—
so I couldn't help it.
I picked it up and put Melli's foot in it, and it fit.
I stood back and said,
feet are kind of ugly until you put shoes on them
and they become art.

Then the clerk said, can I help you?

I said, do thee have these in black?
and he said, I'll check,
and as soon as he was gone
Melli put on her own shoe
and we emptied our bags of stolen shoes onto the sofa
and I said goodbye to little red Isabella
and we walked away.

I felt better, so better, right away,
better even than in church,
like my bones didn't ache anymore,
and my eyes weren't leaking
and my brain was juiced up a little,
and I felt better, swinging empty bags.
I said, Melli, if you want an angel
you've got to fast from stolen shoes,
deny yourself ungodly platforms.
And if I get an angel, you're going home.

Call didn't notice
that I had made Restitution.

He was reading the paper when we got back,
like a responsible citizen.
He said, without putting down the paper,
I knew I could trust you—
you buy some nice shoes?
I said, no, I don't believe in shoes anymore.
I said, here's your money back,
invest in the business.

He said, I knew you loved me,
now get out there, get to work.
He said, when are you going to turn her out?
are you sick of earning for two yet?
are you sure you don't want your candy?

I said, never, no, yes, I am sure.

I wore my see-through plastic flip-flops
that matched and were bought by my mom,
and me and Melli went to the gate of ten thousand happinesses,
and I knew something was going to happen
because of Restitution.

Widow said,
not you again,
not your twinkie again, oh lord.

Widow said, go ahead and die then,
and stop breathing my air.
Here I stopped swearing around you,
see if I don't start again,
see if I don't . . .

She said, hey, that's fine,
more people to lose the Mr. P lottery.
If it's you, it's not me.

I said,
    Diana?
    Debra?
    Dorothy?
    Ingrid?

and she said,
    no
    no
    no
    Ingrid? no

I said, Widow, don't worry,
something is going to happen.
I made Restitution.

And then John the john drove up
and Serena in my head saying, see? see?

I said, Melli, stay here with Widow,
don't talk to strangers
and just say no to drugs.

After the handwipe
I started reading for John,
and I felt tired but so better—
I read and read and this time
the first sentence I read made sense.
The first sentence and the next one
and the next.

I knew what it all meant, every word,
and I read it with red-hot punctuation
and I read it with grammar
and John, his eyes were melty—

But strange
Hath been the cause, and wonderful to hear:
This Tree is not as we are told, a tree
Of danger tasted, nor to evil unknown
Op'ning the way, but of divine effect
To open eyes, and make them gods who taste.

My eyes saw the words 3-D, jumpy on the page,
pick-up-able, like I could peel them back
and find myself underneath
in a whole flat world, white, I-D,
but me.

I stopped, said,
I get it now . . .

John said, I can tell.
He said, so now you see how the world
is the woman's fault, the weaker, the impure sex,
vain and in need of rule.

I said, but it was a setup—
what did they expect?
even the angels couldn't see through the bad guy's disguise . . .
she didn't know what it was to die
she didn't know what evil was
she didn't know what disobey was
she was too pure, too innocent,
it doesn't count . . .

I said, louder and louder,
what's so bad about knowledge anyway?
I said, didn't God make that tree? that fruit?
why? because he wanted them to grow up to be like him,
because it would have been a boring story without it,
that's why!
because they couldn't really love until she did it—
Eve did it for love . . .

Maybe he had a plan,
maybe it was a setup, a plan . . .
maybe it was the way he wanted it.

John frowned.
He said, you are an ignorant girl,
said, I can't expect that a girl like you would know anything,
said, I have been wasting my time . . .
said, you're nothing but a whore
and it's your own fault.

I said, that's the word you call me,
but I am writing my own book of life
and I say you are an old man and hateful,
you wear weird glasses and thick,
I like not you,
give me my money.

He gave me a little,
and I said, more, more—lots, or rip I up your book.

So he gave me more and more,
said, you've spoiled everything,
you won't see me again.

I said, terrific.

When I got out of that car,
there was terrific Melli standing there,
little girl all gold, all quiet smiles,
and nothing was her fault
and I knew something true.
I was smiling with the knowledge of it—
that if you say the word whore
you can make a girl into something,
but she can make words do things, too.

I smiled to know
that you can't see a thing
unless you put on words like glasses.
Everything is just a wobbly vision without a word,
something at the side of your eyes.

Someone can turn you into a stone statue
for everyone to stare at,
but they can never take away
that moustache you drew on it.

I said, Widow,
I figured out how to not be bossed around
by other people's words,
and Widow, in my own story,
I am now going to name you . . . Paula.

Widow looked at me
and she looked up and she said,
Paula.

She said, Paula.
Paula.
She said, I like it—
Paula Paula Paula . . .

and then

just then

Someone was on Widow
right there in the street.

He pushed her down, punched her—
I screamed stop stop but he had her down—
I wrapped my arms around Melli
her mouth open lips pulled back
but no sound
and no sound from the punching
not like TV
no sound
just Widow's air coming out of her—
Widow wouldn't scream for him
wouldn't cry for him
wouldn't beg . . .

I let go of Melli, said run run
but she didn't run
just stood with her mouth open
and nothing coming out.

I stopped the next car,
ran in front of it,
said, call 911 please please please

and then I ran my whole self right over that line,
I screamed for Widow, stop! stop!
I kicked him hard, but he was so high on hurting her
that he didn't feel it, not a thing,
except how good he felt for hurting her
his face loose with pleasure . . .

The police pulled up
quiet, calm ...
and right away the guy was up off Widow and running ...

Widow looked at me, her eyes like bullets,
her mouth bleeding, but her eyes saying,
don't you cry
don't you feel sorry for me
don't you, girl.

The police pulled up
and I bent over Widow
who was bleeding down her legs
and out of her nose
and her face had teeth marks on it.

Widow was all eyes for me
and she smiled with blue lips
and blood teeth
and I touched her forehead,
said, Paula.

The police
pushed me aside
and one said to Widow, stand up, get up, get up,
and she did, loose, like a bag of bones
and they put handcuffs on her.

He went that way, I shouted, that way,
you could catch him!

But they didn't chase him.
Instead they dragged Widow to the car,
and one put his hands on her breasts
as he pushed her in.

I leaned on the car door
and she said angels
and I said no
and she said yes
and I said no that is dumb,
said it with the last of my brains
running out of my eyes—

She smiled a hard smile,
a smile with teeth like stones,
and she said,
don't you let this hurt you, baby,
she said,
you owe me a toe.

I said, you are smart, Paula,
no angels here, no tricky corners—

But she smiled her blood at me,
said, don't you let them do that to you,
and I had to step back fast
so the car wouldn't run over my feet.

I turned
and Melli
still there, still there—
too scared to run.

Another policeman was standing between me and her—
he had a nice police tie pin,
and he said, I'll take you home.

My hips felt out of joint again
like I was having a big baby get born out of me.

The officer said, my name is Dave.

I said, are you arresting me?
He pointed at Melli and said, she should be in bed.
He said, come on, let's go.

I said, you don't know where I live,
but he did.

Call was there when we got back,
surprised to see me so early in the evening
and scared to see me with police,
but Dave said, I'd like a word.

The whole time they talked
so quiet and respectful
I held Melli's hand and thought of Widow
I mean Paula
and I thought—
I thought,
but I did Restitution.

Call and the policeman talked about how this is just business
and all the do-gooders in the world
are the real cause of all the trouble.
Call talked about his business intentions
and then Dave shook Call's hand,
said he understood the way the world is,
and Call shook back and said,
first time for free.

Call said to me, this is Dave
and you do whatever he tells you.

I said to Dave, in the bedroom where Melli can't see.

In the bedroom I said,
will Widow be okay, officer?

He said, call me Daddy—Daddy Dave.

I thought, Widow, Paula,
would be happy when she got back to the midtrack
if I could tell her I said this thing,
this one thing.

So I said,
if you were my real daddy
I would say someone is getting the girls,
they are not missing, they are dead.

I said, everyone knows someone gone,
someone who has kids
but doesn't call them anymore,
someone who loves her sister
but doesn't visit anymore,
someone who had money under a mattress
and it's still there . . .

Daddy Dave snorted, said,
keeping track of you all is like herding chickens—
you leave, your boyfriends take you out.
What do you expect?
He said,
show me a body—
you got one under the bed?
and then he smiled and said,
I'm not here for work.

He said, we're going to play the word game,
and he was fancy with words
but not as good as Milton's 630,
not as good as
dismissive
unprincipled.

He threw the words around, beat them all bruisey
and made me eat them,
made me say things, made me speak un-angel,
put words in my ears, stuffed them in far,
and made them come out of my mouth.
All those black and blue words made me sick,
my stomach full of mouldy brown words.
He beat the words up, twisted them.

But he didn't know about my book of life
and how later I would brush the words off,
break them into letters like bread
and put them in a poem.

When he was finished Daddy Dave said,
don't worry, I might be assigned
to head up the task force
for the investigation of the missing women.
The last one got caught
with pornography on his work computer.

He said, see you.

Right after he left, I got out my book of life
and wrote it all down
about Widow, about Paula,

about how the story kept turning out not how I meant,
not how I meant at all—

I closed my book.

I went out to the broken-bone couch to find Melli

but she was gone.

And so was Call.

Submitting to what seemed remediless . . .

Call brought her back,
boneless and broken,
her eyes speaking the same language as her mouth.

He handed her the cards, said, play,
but she held them in her hand and didn't play.

I said, what did you do? what have you done?

Call said, she's been to the baby dentist.

He said, if you're going to give me trouble, Angel,
you tell me now,
tell me straight.
You want to walk out that door, you go.
I've got Melli now, and she's fresh, you know?
So go if you want . . .

I knew I wouldn't make it to the end of the block.
I knew he would be so mad that I would really leave him,
I knew if I made it to the end of the block
he would hurt Jeremy—kill Jeremy—
I knew it while I stared at Melli,
while I couldn't believe what he had done.

I couldn't leave Melli anyway.

I said, evil Call, where would I go?
who would want me?

He nodded, looked at me with hurt in his eyes
because he knew I stayed for Melli.

He said, don't call me that,
don't call me evil.
He said, you should be afraid of me.

I said, okay, evil Call.
You want fear,
okay, I can do that.
I can do it excellent,
stand straight under it,
salute it,
artistify it.

Call picked up the cards,
said, I'll show you a game, Melli.
I'll show you a trick.

He said, pick a card and look at it,
but don't show me—
now put it on your forehead
and I'll read your mind.

She didn't want to play,
sitting on the broken-bone couch,
but she did what he said,
and he guessed the card.

He said, want to know the trick?
Want to know how I did that?
She didn't nod, her whole body was silent—

He put a finger on her skull
and said, there's no trick.
I can read your mind for real.
I'll know if you ever think a thought
about leaving me.

He said, I've got a late meeting with gentry,
and he went out and locked us in.

When he was gone,
I got out my book
and I went slow and quiet to the couch
and I said, slow and quiet, Melli, I have magic, too.
My book hides secrets, in code: a b c d
abracadabra—sleight of word,
letters up my sleeve.
Call never checks sleeves, Melli.
I'll find a noun behind your ear,
and make the meaning disappear—

but nothing made her smile.

I said, I'm sorry, Melli.
I said, there has to be the possibility of sad endings
or there couldn't be such a thing as happy endings.
Endings are happy because they could have been sad.
Maybe ours will be sad.

When I said that
Melli leaned forward,
hunched up, curled in,
made herself small
until her shoulder blades flattened and disappeared
into the round of her back
and her wing places vanished into herself—

I knew why the baby dentist wanted to do it.
It was an angel he wanted.
If she was dead and cold, he wouldn't want her.
But inside her, maybe an angel
who warmed her up, lit her up, made her hum—
it was her he wanted.
He wanted to suck out her light till he glowed in the dark.

I put my finger to her cheek and tasted her tear,
thinking to swallow light,
a little star to pour on your cereal in the morning . . .

But no—just a tear.

She was just a little girl.

And then I couldn't stand it, Melli's silence,
and I shouted, speak!
say something!
But she just cried more
and I couldn't believe I did that,
and I promised and promised I'd never do it again,
said, sorry, sorry . . .
I hugged her and said, it's okay,
you don't have to talk—I don't care.

I said to Melli, don't you know how cute you are?
You are a spirity supermodel, a beauty queen boo,
a cutie patootie cream cheese pattycake babycake you—
you are specialer than special . . .

I said, I'm writing a story about you
and in it the baby dentist dies a gruesome gory death
upside down in a dentist's chair
poked all over with needles and drills.

She didn't smile
but she let me tuck her into bed.

Next day I made food for Melli,
biscuits and milk and scrambled egg whites,
but she wouldn't eat, only drank the milk,
and she held the cards
but she wouldn't play.

Call and Asia left to collect more names
the whole time thinking up plans,
all dumb.

And Melli wouldn't play,
so I played cards while Melli watched.

I heard the key in the door,
but it wasn't Call, it was Daddy Dave,
and he said, Call knows I'm here.

In the bedroom I said,
how is Widow?

He said, she died.
She died of a bleed in the drunk tank.

I said, just a moment.

I went into the kitchen
and got Call's knife out of the drawer
and I took off my shoe and I held the knife
over my toe,
held it with my hand pushing down
and my toe pushing up,
my hand wanting to make it up for Widow
for Paula Paula Paula
who forgot her name that's how bad it was.
But there was no Restitution big enough
for her being dead,
and my toe pushing up
and my hand pushing down
I heard Widow's voice saying,
don't you let them do that to you—
and then Melli came in and put her hollow bone hand
on mine
and took the knife away.

That Melli.

I said, Melli, you won't go back to the baby dentist
because—because I'm going to get a plan.

Saying it was belief enough

because right then I got one.
A plan.

I whispered to Melli,
holding the knife,
I think I know a way
to make Daddy Dave take you home—
I know a way
so Call will think it was Daddy Dave's idea
and Jeremy won't get hurt.

I took the knife out of her hand
and she was scared but I said, it's okay,
and I made Daddy Dave a sandwich, ham,
and I took it to the bedroom
where Melli couldn't see
and I said to Daddy Dave with a ham sandwich,
too bad you let Widow die, too bad.

I watched Daddy Dave bite into his sandwich
and chew and chew
as if there were bones in that ham
or rubbery bits of eyeball—
his ham sandwich rolled around and around
in his mouth while we chatted
and I was ever so nice.

I said, at least she didn't get killed by Mr. P.

He said, with his mouth full of ham,
you can't go saying there's a killer out there.
Scares all the law-abiding folks
who just want to eat their dinner in peace.
They don't know about your world,
and they don't want to.
Now Angel, you ask yourself, dig down deep,
what kind of life did those women have anyway?
Ever think of it that way?

I thought, he deserves my plan.

I watched him chew
with my toe still quivering
and Paula dead in the drunk tank
and Melli in the kitchen
and me knowing my plan.

Then we played the dirty word game
and I found a way to tip out his wallet—

he never saw, he was so taken with his little girl, that's me,
that's how we play.

And after that, and after the part where he cries
because he feels so bad, I kicked the wallet away
under the bed,
and after the part where he looks at me and says it isn't fair
and the part where I have to comfort him—

after that he didn't have any money to pay.
Surprise!

I cried,
I said, Call is going to kill me if I don't get some money,
he's not going to believe it,
which was sort of true so I didn't lie, top ten.

I cried some more and I said,
he's going to think you're pulling one over on him,
and I cried more, and Daddy Dave said
shut up, shut up—
he said, tell Call I'll pay you double next time—

I said, give me your watch to prove it,
and he did.

I said, give me your tie pin, too—
(it says twenty years with a police crest on it)
and he said no, and I cried,
not even fake crying 'cause I was so scared of my plan,
and he said shut up
and gave it to me, said, tell Call I'll pay him next time . . .

He left without his wallet ha ha
and his watch
and his tie pin,
which I hid all of them under the mattress.

And after that Call,
sudden and loud,
saying I have an interview with a reporter tomorrow—
he heard about our petition
and wants to write an article on us—
we're going to be news—
can you believe it, Angel?
It could be so good for us soon,
just have faith in me,
and he hugged me and said,
don't leave me, Angel, don't leave,
and he meant, don't make me kill you.

I said, look, Call, look,
and I gave him the money
I'd taken out of Daddy Dave's wallet,
there was lots extra,
so I said, this is for two.
Call said, good business, Angel-girl,
and I said, I'm all about customer service.
He kissed me and carried me to bed
and he ground out some tribal—

but under the mattress,
there with my book of life
the watch
the wallet
the tie pin
the plan . . .

How are we happy, still in fear of harm?

Today is the day, Call said.

He practiced reporter questions with Asia.

Asia said, what if he asks you how would you advertise?

Call said, the Dutch have display windows—you can get any size, color. It's much safer for the customer.

Yes, said Asia, pretending to be the reporter, but isn't it true that in the Netherlands the number of child prostitutes has tripled since legalization?

Call said, I don't see the connection. Isn't it all just harmless fun? Just think about all those girls competing for your business—the possibilities.

Call and Asia laughed at that one.

Asia said, okay, get serious here, how will you staff your business?

Call said, it's an employment option for the poor.

Call said, did I do good?

I said, wow, Call.

It's going to be all good from here, Angel,
I promise,
we'll start new.

I said, I know, it's true.
I said, if you don't lock us in, I'll get groceries
and cook you something red
to celebrate.

He hugged me and left, wearing good clothes
and carrying his names in his almost empty briefcase
and leaving the door unlocked
and the rhino guarding the door.

I had to wake Melli up
and she didn't want to—
she wanted to stay in her dreams
where she didn't know Call or me.

She woke up silent as a kitten,
yawned silent,
and I said, today is the day.

I pushed off the mattress
and there
my book
the wallet
the watch
the pin—
and Serena's envelope.

The envelope was full of Serena's going-home money.
I put it in my pocket and said,
thanks, dead Serena.

I stuck the tie pin in my book of life,
stabbed right into a blank page,
and the book with the pin and Daddy Dave's wallet and watch
and Serena's money
went in my almost empty purse
and I said, here comes the end of the story, Melli—
here we go.
I said, don't be scared.
Call says police like doughnuts—
I bet they have doughnuts, hey Melli?
You like doughnuts, Melli?

We walked to the Police Station,
capital P capital S,
and the rain fell like tinsel,
each drip a ray in the dusk,
each splashed into puddles like moons,
made slow-motion flowers of light
that rain from the sea,
still with salt in it,
still smelling of shark,
my boughten flip-flops spangled with droplets
like sequins—

I walked with Melli holding my hand.

We passed the Jimi Hendrix shrine,
him singing about a girl who walks through the clouds
and rides with the wind
and says take anything you want from me—

and when we couldn't hear him anymore
I talked to Melli about how
maybe an angel could be around any corner,
corners could be tricky like that,
and that's all I needed to be happy,
was the odd suspicious-looking corner.

I said, we're almost there.
Don't worry, it's my story now.

At the front door of the Police Station
were receptionists behind bulletproof glass,
up high like queens, grumpy queens,
so we went out and walked around looking for other doors
and found where the cop cars were parked—

We found the side door
which needed a swiper card,
so we looked in Daddy Dave's wallet,
and what do you know—

Melli did the swiping
and we walked into the Police Station
bold as can be,
like we were somebody's princesses
like we were girls whose faces
would be on a missing children's poster
like maybe it was supposed to go this way.

A cop, a young one with white hair, said,
what have we got here?

I said, this is Melli Smith.
We're here to see Dave.

He said, got a few Daves here,
why don't you come on in and tell me if yours is here.

We followed the young officer with white hair
and he said, what's your name? and what's your last name?
and is this your sister?
and then we saw Daddy Dave sitting at his desk,
wearing a tie but no pin, ha ha, and no watch.

I pointed.

Daddy Dave looked up and the other cop said our names,
said, these girls say they are looking for you.
Friends of yours?

Daddy Dave went angel-wing white
and pretended not to know us
without his tie pin and his watch.

Melli's hand was shaking, so was mine,
and I said, hey Daddy Dave.
The other cop looked at him hard.
Daddy Dave said, do I know you,
and I said, remember Melli Smith?
I bet she belongs to somebody.
I don't want her to end up with Mr. P.
He stood up and waved his hand for us to come closer.

I said, so the white-haired one couldn't hear,
if you take her home
and tell Call you did it yourself
without it being my idea,
and you will because of this and other reasons—
and I showed him his wallet.
I said, sorry, I have my brother Jeremy to think about.

He said,
I don't know what you're talking about.

I whispered, yes you do because of tie pins.
I said, just take Melli home, please.
I said it ever so polite
because you can do that
when you've got a watch and a wallet and a tie pin.

The white-haired officer had walked away,
and really fast Daddy Dave took us into another room,
and his face white as paper
and not even any words.

He grabbed my purse and dumped it out,
the notebook and Serena's money,
and took his wallet and watch
and held my purse upside down and shook it hard,
said, where's the pin, where's the pin,
said God's name over and over
but this time it was a real prayer.

I said, first Melli . . .
that's all I said.

Where's the tie pin?
He was praying his mouth off,
but I was silent as Melli.

Daddy Dave said, you're in trouble, girl,
you have no idea.

He tried to take Melli, but she held on to me
and I held on to her
and he tried to pry her off
and she squealed one perfect high note.

I said, you don't say much, Melli,
but when you do, it's good.

I said, I have to know she's okay
and you have to tell Call it's your idea
because of my little brother Jeremy.
I said, I'll still play your game,
I'll pat your back when you're done.

Daddy Dave said, if I don't?
I don't want to be on Call's bad side—
I've got family, too, you know.

I said, maybe you will get a plan.
I said, hurry, that man with the white hair,
he's going to wonder how I got your tie pin.

Daddy Dave grabbed my arm hard hard hard
and then he dropped it and went out.

I picked up Serena's money
and my book and put them back in my purse
and we waited.
Melli touched the bruises welting on my arms
and it felt so good to sit with my hand on hers,
but I wasn't just sitting,
I was believing,
I breathed beams.

Daddy Dave came back
and slapped a file on the table.

You think they're going to believe a girl with a record?

He showed me,
and there it was—

shoplifting.

He said, you stole my tie pin.

I said, Serena knew shoes were gonna be the death of me.

I said, I made Restitution.

He said, don't you think they'll know what you are?
Why do you think they'll believe you?
I could arrest you right now for kidnapping,
he said, his voice all shaking like he was dopesick.
You're in trouble.

The white-haired officer came to the door, peeked in,
said to Daddy Dave,
what about that phone call couple days ago
from a lady reverend
about two young girls who came to church—
didn't you say you'd look into that?

The white-haired officer said to Melli,
will you come with me?
To me he said, don't worry, we'll take care of her,
she'll just be in the next room.

I wouldn't have let her go
if he hadn't said that
and if his hair wasn't white
which was just because it was my story now.
I nodded and she went
and I called after, I bet she likes doughnuts.

And then Daddy Dave did a search on me
and there in the Police Station
it was worse than any street.

He did not find the pin, ha ha,
because he was not interested
in reading my book of life,
no he did not care to read,
which was one miracle,
and then another miracle came
after I was dressed
and the white-haired officer poked in his head
and said, we've got something on one Melli Smith,
a photo.
I've put in a call.

He said to Daddy Dave,
this is going to be interesting,
and he left again.

I found out that when you get a miracle,
you don't jump up and down,
you don't scream,
you just relax into a universe that's got your back.
You just want to live and see what happens.

Daddy Dave said, okay, you got what you wanted,
was it worth it?
we'll see what Call has to say about this.

I said, the plan is for you to say
it was my idea, Call,
my idea—
you can't keep little girls like Melli, Call.
Then I'll give you back your pin.

Daddy Dave said, I already phoned Call.
We'll see what he thinks about you now.
We'll see what he does to your brother.
I just lost that pin, you picked it up.
You're just a little thief,
shoes and tie pins,
just a thief.

I looked at him
with the miracle at my back
and Melli almost saved,
and I said, you told Call I was here?
But the tie pin—

I couldn't breathe in that room made for searching,
I couldn't share the air with that man.

I jumped up and grabbed my bag and ran to the door
and Daddy Dave grabbed me
and me fighting back
like I could kill him
never mind God's top ten,
scratching his hands that grabbed me
scratching so I could feel his skin
peeling into my fingernails
and all his dirty words pouring out of his mouth
and me saying, in vain!
and, angel, angel—

then I was out of the room, swallowing air
but not enough—
I couldn't get enough air,
and I could see Melli eating a doughnut, white,
and I could see Call coming toward me
Daddy Dave behind me
saying
there he is
and it's your own fault—

and then

there she was

my angel.

The world was all before them,
where to choose ...

I thought she would be
all floaty and filmy,
all fragile ghost-bones that break,
all dandelion-seed hair and weightless—

but no.
She was stone, fixed, forever . . .

Her words dripped into my ear—
each drop weighed a star.

She said, Angel,
when God reads your book of life,
boy, are some people ever gonna get it.

I said,
Jeremy,
and she said,
Call's pocket,
which I did not understand,
which I thought was angel talk.

I said, I don't want to hurt anymore.

And she said, it will be all pillows.

I was surprised by this angel—

I was surprised by how pale my believing was,
how shrivelled up and shrunk,
how stingy
compared to knowing.

I was surprised by this angel
who said,

see?
see?

And then she was gone.

The angel was gone
and Melli was still holding her white doughnut
and with her big open-mouth smile
and sparkly sugar on her teeth
and she said, "Angel."

She said my name out loud,
made it sound like the prettiest word in the English language
made my name sound like a poem to me.

I said, oh Melli, you poet.

Then Melli pointed to Call
and said something to the white-haired officer,
and the officer looked at Call
which pinned Call to the floor,
Call who was not expecting white-haired officers
and Melli telling on him.

I took out the tie pin
and gave it to Daddy Dave
and said, I'm not a thief,
and the white-haired officer looked at Daddy Dave.

So much looking.

So I looked at Call
in his eyes, right in his eyes,
and I was not scared anymore.

I saw something flicking there,
something electric,
a white wire of light, arcing in the eye—
as if his eye remembered seeing something—

then it was gone,
and all I could see in the juicy part of his eyes
were crusted, burnt things—
but I knew my eyes were filled with floating gold,
and you can't be afraid with eyeballs like that.

Then I looked him right in the shirt pocket
and in the pocket was an envelope
and I slipped the envelope out
and it was the one I sent to Dad
and on it were the letters RTS—
moved—address unknown—
in black marker.

RTS, return to sender,
the prettiest letters in the alphabet.

I said to Call, they moved.
You don't know where Jeremy is anymore.

And I did my invisible angel thing
with everybody looking at Call and Daddy Dave,
and I walked away
right past the grumpy queens
right out the front door
and I walked with Serena's money
and my book of life in my purse
and floating gold in my eyeballs—

I walked to the end of the block
and I walked past the library
and past the phone booth
and into China
and I walked past the Jimi Hendrix shrine,
him singing about the moon and the deep blue sea
and fly on, fly on,
and all the way to the gate of ten thousand happinesses
where I named Widow Paula and it was true—

A van with tinted windows pulled up beside me
drove beside me
while I just kept walking in my boughten flip-flops
and my feet being art as they just kept walking
to they didn't know where or to who—
and the van followed me to a bookstore
where I just walked right in.

I breathed in the books,
the good smell a million books make,
and the bookstore was my home
and the leather reading chair was my chair
and the bookstore clerk loved to see me read.

He smiled, said, can I help you?
I said, yes, do thy have paradise lost?
and he said, come this way
and I came
and he did.

I bought my own copy of paradise lost
with Serena's money and said, good job, dead Serena,
and I sat in my chair by my window
and turned to the last book of paradise lost
to the very last book, book twelve,
and nobody could stop me.

The clerk circling around the store
always ending up at my chair
watching me read book twelve
and the van outside circling around the block
and me reading where Adam and Eve get told a story
in which they were the beginning of stories,
and the world was all before them—

All the world. It said that.
It said in book twelve
that all the world was before them
and they could choose . . .

Author's Note

Angel, Serena, Melli, Widow, Call and Daddy Dave are my own invention. But inside my made-up story is much that is true.

It is true that a young girl is commonly lured into prostitution because the man she thinks is her boyfriend turns out to be a pimp. Sometimes he is the one who introduces her to street drugs. Often, once she is "turned out," she takes drugs to help her tolerate the lifestyle. She stays for many reasons: because she must feed her addiction, because she is afraid she will be beaten or killed if she leaves, or because her pimp has threatened to hurt her family members if she leaves. Each girl's story is different.

It is true that, beginning in 1983, a number of women disappeared from Vancouver's Downtown Eastside, an area notorious for its poverty, open drug use and high rate of HIV infection—one of the highest in the world. Most but not all of the women who vanished from the Eastside were sex workers. Over the next thirteen years, families and friends filed missing-persons reports, giving reasons why they thought their loved ones were not just missing but dead. Nothing was done.

In 1997, the same year that eleven more women went missing, Robert William "Willy" Pickton handcuffed and attacked a sex worker, who fled naked with knife wounds to her stomach. The charges against Pickton were stayed, however, because the sex worker was not considered a reliable witness. She cannot be named because a court ban prohibits using her real name.

In 1998, an additional ten women went missing. Police were told that bloody clothing and a number of women's purses, complete with ID, had been seen lying around Pickton's farm.

That same year the Vancouver Police Department issued a news release saying that law enforcement officers did not believe a serial killer was behind the disappearances.

By the time Pickton was arrested in 2002, nineteen more women had been reported missing. Investigators found on his farm the remains and the DNA of thirty-two of the missing women. Pickton admitted to the murders of forty-nine women; he was convicted of six counts of second-degree murder and sentenced to life in prison with no chance of parole for twenty-five years.

I respectfully acknowledge that the names I use on pages 49 and 117 refer to several of the real missing women: Debra Jones, Dawn Crey, Dianne Rock, Sarah de Vries and Janet Henry.

The Missing Women of Vancouver's Downtown Eastside*

Yvonne Abigosis

Sereena Abotsway

Sharon Abraham

Elaine Allenbach

Angela Arseneault

Sherry Baker

Cindy Beck

Yvonne Boen

Andrea Borhaven

Heather Bottomley

Heather Chinnock

Nancy Clark

Wendy Crawford

Marcella Creison

Dawn Crey

Sarah de Vries

Sheryl Donahue

Tiffany Drew

Elaine Dumba

Sheila Egan

Cara Ellis

Gloria Fedyshyn

Cynthia Feliks

Marnie Frey

Jennifer Furminger

Catherine Gonzalez

Rebecca Guno

Michelle Gurney

Inga Hall

Helen Hallmark

Ruby Hardy

Janet Henry

Tanya Holyk

Sherry Irving

Angela Jardine

Andrea Joesbury

Patricia Johnson

Debra Jones

Catherine Knight

Kerry Koski

Marie Laliberte

Stephanie Lane

Danielle Larue

Kellie Little

Verna Littlechief

Laura Mah

Jacquelene McDonell

Diana Melnick

* Sources: missingpeople.net and Missing Women Task Force list, 2007

Leigh Miner
Marilyn Moore
Jackie Murdock
Georgina Papin
Tania Petersen
Sherry Rail
Dianne Rock
Elsie Sebastian
Ingrid Soet
Dorothy Spence

Teresa Triff
Sharon Ward
Kathleen Wattley
Olivia Williams
Taressa Williams
Mona Wilson
Brenda Wolfe
Frances Young
Julie Young

Thanks

I wish to express my deep gratitude to Candace Fisher, Sarah Gough, Stephen Roxburgh, Julie Larios and Brenda Bowen, who gave me guidance and much-needed encouragement as I wrote this book. I am always grateful to my family, who inspire me in my work. I am especially indebted to my brilliant editors Margaret Ferguson and Shelley Tanaka. Thanks also to the Alberta Foundation for the Arts and the Canada Council for the Arts for their timely support.

Martine Leavitt